In the Palm of the Left Hand Black

Damien Casey
Art by Christopher McCormick
Ig- @csm1321

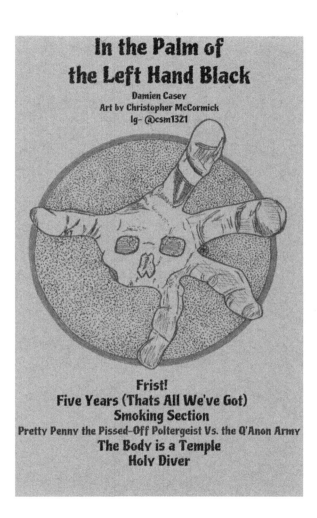

Frist!
Five Years (Thats All We've Got)
Smoking Section
Pretty Penny the Pissed-Off Poltergeist Vs. the Q'Anon Army
The Body is a Temple
Holy Diver

A LITTLE THINGY THING BEFORE YOU DIVE IN

I'm going to center his text... because I want to!

The following six stories are just some stories that I enjoyed writing immensely and just really want to share.

I love the Cloverfield movies, this has nothing to do with anything.

I really loved how Adam Green released Victor Crowley without telling anyone he was even working on it.

So, I'm sorry to my closest friends who always get to read my stuff before it's even been properly edited.

It's hard to read this the way I centered it, but it's a choice I have made, and I guess I'll stick with it.

I also really wanted to do something with Chris Mccormick.

His art is perfectly minimal and makes me smile every time it shows up in my feed.

Chris is a constant and great supporter of authors like me.

He is always posting our books, making us into stupid ghosts, and just being there for the conversations with a good friend.

Chris Mccormick rulzzzzz

I hope you enjoy the stories.

I hope Chris' art brings you the smiles it brings me.

K thx

FRIST!

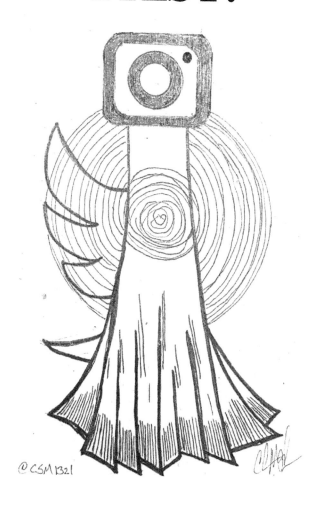

@ CSM 1321

I sit in my padded room with a pen and a pad of post-It notes. They took away my permanent markers; as a side effect of my state of madness, I have taken to writing indecipherable scrolls on every inch of white I can find upon the walls. I was not prohibited a spiral notebook as I had asked, the orderly said the metal coil presented a risk. I fear the man has no true sense of the word "risk" if he observes a metal coil with the same reverence as should be reserved for the lurking, nameless fears of one's own mind. I was also infatuated with his oversight of the pen, which could be much more damaging than the coil in question!

I would request whoever finds these notes slapped against the wall to distrust a translation from my handwriting to a digital document. Some words I have written reference ancient, timeless beings who only need to see their name ran through the autocorrect of an iPhone to devour your very essence and send your mind spiraling into madness.

My story starts on a cold and dreary September day. I was in my bed, covered up to my shoulders trying to avoid any mention of responsibility. I scrolled endlessly through apps like Twitter and Instagram. Instagram, in my opinion, being the better app. I prefer the photo-based platform of Instagram as opposed to the text-dominant Twitter.

Neither of which have I been able to access in months! Yet do I feel my madness subside? The opposite! This madness is like a fattened tick growing in my mind, feasting upon any remnant of rational thought in my brain. On this day, I was paying attention to something particular that had caught my attention; I had seen the comment "first!" left as the first comment on a number of celebrities' photos. What was the endgame here? What was the purpose? My mind searched for an answer as if it were a guppy in Arizona looking for the Atlantic. I became fascinated, obsessed! I scrolled to the top of the app and refreshed over and over again until a post from Meghan Trainor popped up. One second ago! Now was my time to unlock the secrets of being the first commenter! My fingers moved quickly over six buttons to type my message, I hurriedly hit the send button.

There it was.

I had done it.

"Frist!"

Madness had struck me. In my urgency to beat all the other competitors, I had misspelled the word! My finger hovered over my phone's screen; do I delete the comment? I asked myself, equally afraid of losing this small joy but equally terrified that I would be insulted for my spelling error.

The comments began to appear in response to mine.

5

"Oof"

"Learn how to spell, Dickhead."

"Technically my comment was first because you spelled it wrong."

And a simple, to the point message of "fuck you."

It was a scene from Frankenstein in which my comment was the misunderstood creation, and the responders were the angry villagers coming to burn me alive in the lighthouse! (A side note: There is a deleted scene from the movie in which Frankenstein's monster walks to the window of the lighthouse before it collapses and says "Hello, Angry Villagers! Before I die, I just wanted you to know that it is ok to refer to me as simply 'Frankenstein', as saying 'Frankenstein's monster' every time you mention me is quite lengthy, annoying, and you will come across as a pretentious ass.") I began to sweat with worry, what if Meghan Trainor herself had seen my comment! What if she was sitting at a table somewhere with her husband and friends, all of them laughing at my spelling error and discussing a plan to make sure I was never anything more than a laughingstock again!

The sheer madness led me to delete my comment, the damage was already done I was sure, but maybe with self-awareness, I could salvage the situation.

I sighed and checked my notifications, hoping the endless line of responses would stop. I had gained a new follower, Nihilartikle. I touched his profile picture and was guided to his page; I assume this user to be a "he" as the manner of things I was bear witness to on this page had to come from the mind of a darkly twisted man!

Also, he had a couple of selfies.

As I scrolled through post and post of indescribable horrors my mind said, "Stop looking!" But my eyes craved more. My eyes had become an endlessly chewing mouth with an insatiable appetite for the crimes of misspelled words on the internet.

Every post was a person like me, someone who had used a spelling error, misused punctuation, used a run-on sentence, and all other matters of blasphemy to the God of the English language. Comments under each post picking up where the others had left off, endless and unspeakable humiliation.

I refreshed the page praying to the god of stupid things people do on the internet to allow my sin to go unpunished.

My prayers went unanswered.

There it was, a picture of my comment and a caption that read "You can delete the comment but not my screenshot!"

Below their work had begun again, comments upon comments. I shrunk into myself, I could feel insanity wrapping itself around my neck like a rope, I could feel my breath shortening, I was filled with panic.

I frantically clicked the follow button on the page and typed a message pleading that my post be removed. The response I received goes as follows.

"What an absolute dord you are! The Mountweazel of Abacot and The Cairbow of Kime look upon your name in shame."

What kind of response was that for a person to send to another person? I quickly typed a response. "Please! I seek guidance! Have remorse upon me! I did not know what I was doing, I am guilty of an innocent crime."

"The crime you have committed is far from innocent! Much like every other human let loose to pollinate this realm of the internet you have committed a crime against me, The God of English and Grammar! Your torment will never end! You will feel a humiliation so deep that you will look over everything you type with the care of a mother holding her newly born child."

"There must be a way to avoid such tortures. Not even the most Damned of the damned deserve a punishment like this. I will spend eons upon eons of time looking at what I have already said!"

"Blasphemer! Even now you have committed a crime in the word 'eons', you have used a singular word as a plural! The correct word for your statement is 'aeons'!"

"Are you sure?"

"You dare to question me?"

"No! No! Not at all! Please forgive me! I was just asking, so I didn't, you know, do it again."

"Oh, ok, well enough. You appear to be a man who wants to right his wrongs, so this time only I will allow a reprieve!"

"Yes! Anything! Please!"

"You must reach out to the person who made the post you committed blasphemy upon, you must be granted permission by this person to take them to the Phantomnation with you in an act of momblishness."

"Sure. I don't know what any of that means, but, sure."

"The person must accept the invitation!"

I had to be free of this unseen force that sought to destroy me! I commented on every one of Meghan Trainor's posts saying, "I beg you to accompany me to the Phantomnation in an act of momblishness." I knew not, and still know not what I was asking, I just sought a yes.

After a time, I found I could no longer access her Instagram profile! I had been blocked! I am sure many people leave ten or more comments on every photo just like I did, was Nihilartikle working against me?

I did the same on Twitter hoping to outwit him. He beat me to it and I was blocked after only one hundred tweets and messages! I searched Facebook and did the same. Damn! I was blocked again! TikTok? Blocked! I began to do the same to her husband's profiles, blocked again!
In the highest severity of my insanity, I had located a distant cousin with only fifty followers and begun begging her to convince Meghan to accompany me to the Phantomnation in an act of momblishness, it was at this point I had heard a knock upon my door. I answered and a local police officer was before me, he told me he was to stop by and talk to me about online harassment and do a wellness check. I explained to him how commenting "Frist!" had committed me to a life of torture at the hands of Nihilartikle! I explained my dire situation with The Mountweazel of Abacot and The Cairbow of Kime gazing upon the letters in my name with disappointment. I explained my quest at great length. He stepped outside in silence, the fool clearly realizing he was out of his league!
A half-hour later I was disturbed by another knock, this time two men asking me to accompany them to their vehicle. I refused! I refused quite adamantly! "I adamantly refuse to leave this home!" I yelled at them, we got into a tussle before I felt a pinprick in my arm. In my last moments of consciousness, I heard

one of the men say to the other "Did you know the word 'adamant' actually used to mean something like 'very hard stone?'"

I awoke in the room that is still mine and only mine knowing those men were agents of Nihilartikle sent to claim me. Sent to drag me to this place where I shall suffer madness for the rest of my life. I hear them arguing about the pen now, one of them saw me using it and confronted the man responsible for this oversight. I must stop now as I can hear the steps drawing closer to reclaim this tool. My tale is told. I leave these notes on the wall hoping this person will take them and show the world. The world has to know to never commit such an act as I did when I commented in haste. Humanity must not meddle with things beyond their understanding and if one does… at least check the spelling first.

NOTES:
Imagine if dumb old Lovecraft had social media. Do you think he'd be liking pics of people at the beach and commenting things like "DAGON LIVES!" or do you think he'd be arguing with people on Facebook? Probably a little of both. His profile pic would definitely be some odd from the chin up angled photo of himself.

FIVE YEARS (THAT'S ALL WE'VE GOT)

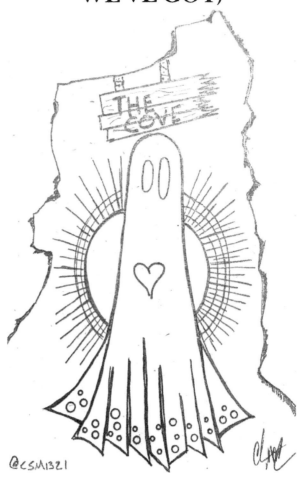

@CSM1321

She wakes up sweating. She rolls out of bed and into the water. The area that used to be farmland that she called home for the night has become a lake with a few floating islands here and there. Quite the opposite of land with a couple small ponds here and there as it was years ago.

She looks out at the horizon and sees what used to be great mountains, mountains that now barely rise twenty feet out of the water. The trees all along these hills are strong and healthy in the trunk, but withered and dry by the top. Leaves crunch from the slightest breeze, raining down like ash from a fire. The water sits calmly between the massive hills, flooding creeks to the point they become rivers.

She dunks her head under water to get rid of the last remnants of sleep still in her body. She crawls along the bank of the hill she was sleeping on last night. Her air mattress was already starting to float.

It wouldn't be long now; it was too hot as it was now. What did they say before the TV stopped working? Five years, right? Give or take, she thinks, but who can really put that distinct of a timer on the Earth's distance from the sun? Was someone out there with a tape measure every day? Was there a news reporter there too? "Hi there, it's

13

Bill Hills reporting for the channel three news, yeaaaahhhhh I'm gonna guess about three more years until we all burn up like an ice cube sitting in the Sahara." Life wasn't that convenient. No one had any idea.

She thought about how frustrated she was about losing her backpack a few months ago. She had everything in it, a dozen cans of green beans, her outdoor thermometer, her knife, and of course a change of clothes.

The good thing about being this damn close to the water all the time, she thinks, *is at least when I wake up, I can wash myself and my clothes before I smell either.*

She sits on the hill deflating the mattress, the black plastic coating has started to get hot enough that it is sticky. Has to be over one-twenty today, she thinks as she rolls the mattress up and places it in the cloth sack she carries it in. The only good thing about losing the backpack was having room in the kayak for this mattress when she found it; sure beat the hell out of sleeping on the hot grass. She wasn't about to attempt sleeping half in and half out of the water like she had before ever again.Last time, she woke up coughing up water, she was convinced something pulled her under but didn't stay long enough to find out. Every part of the earth is like the rainforest now, she had decided, probably an alligator or something.

A few hours pass trying to catch a fish. The fish have become accustomed to living in the deeper waters, or so she guesses because there is a distinct lack of them. It doesn't help that she's trying to do so with her bare hands. She can't face the idea that maybe they're all dying out so any excuse will do.

She walks over the small hill to the kayak she tied up last night using the tent stake she found a week ago. Good thing too, because otherwise she would have had to beat that feral dog the other day with just her bare hands. The other good thing about all this water is it's easy to clean a tent stake after you use it for self-defense so that the blood doesn't cook onto its surface and start to stink up what little existence you have. She sighs to herself. The sound almost startles her. She hasn't made a sound with her mouth in at least a week. Sure, she screamed and yelled fighting the dog, sure she grunts as she struggles to grip a fish, sure she sobs while she cries thinking about her parents' makeshift graves miles under the water surface, but these sounds aren't on purpose. These sounds escape from her like small wounds, each one a new scar she's released from herself into the world. No sound has escaped her mouth just for the sake of sound in far too long.

"Too hot." She says out loud smiling. "Too hot to say or do anything other than what I need to." She shakes her head already regretting speaking.

Is this insanity?

Can the heat cause someone to go completely batshit crazy?

She stops this train of thought and pushes off the grassy hill. She rows slowly for a few miles, taking up most of the day. Just coasting at a leisurely pace, trying to find a shaded area to try and sleep in tonight.

She sees a flash of light up ahead, like the bright sun is reflecting on a floating piece of metal. It wouldn't be the first time she's came across a capsized boat, she slept inside the upside-down dining room of a cruise ship once. *Why did I ever leave that place?* She thinks, *oh yeah, The Junkers.*

She calls them Junkers, but what they are is desperate lonely people. People who have bonded together over nothing more than counting down the days until the planet Earth either turns into an oven baking their skins, or the oceans start to boil and cook everyone like lobsters. A sort of cult is what they are, they find survivors and indoctrinate them into their way of life. The bad part about their way of life is being forced to live in the salt water, the oceans have little to no distinction from the rest of the water now, unless you're in the mountains like she is. The oceans are brutal, sharks stay at the surface, some weird new things have even come up from the bottom.

16

She can't explain that, she doesn't even know if it's real or just something they told her. Either way, no thank you, I'll stay all by myself and not fuck around and find out on the high seas with you nutters.

It's definitely a reflection. She sees a person rowing, a shirtless man with his back to her rowing in her direction. As she gets close enough, she splashs water at him, "Michael Snyder?" She yells almost jumping from her kayak with excitement.

The brown-haired man, with the deeply tanned yet malnourished body spins around in a surprise. "Denise Carpenter?" He yells with the same enthusiasm. "Where have you been? I haven't seen you since...."

"The week before spring break. Calculus."

"Yeah.... Some memory."

"Calculus? I wish I didn't remember it."

"No, remembering the last time we saw each other."

"Oh."

"Oh."

They sit there beside each other, saying nothing, bathing in the silence that can only be created by two people who haven't spoken to another human in years.

"So," he tries to snap the awkwardness, "you're coming from that way?"

"Uh huh."

"Oh."

"Yeah..... no Junkers or anything, just hills."

"What's a Junker?"

"Those crazy ocean people."

"Oh."

"Oh."

"Pirates."

"Them too?"

"No, that's what I call the ocean people."

"Oh."

"Did you see it back there? Is it a hoax?"

"See what?"

"You don't know?"

"Would I act this dumb on purpose?"

"Dolphins?"

"Huh? No, PURPOSE, would I act this dumb on PURPOSE?"

"Oh, sorry, I heard porpoise."

"Are there some close?"

"No.... I mean I thought.... we both have our brains filled with hot water."

"Sometimes I think my brain is a giant ravioli boiling in the pot of my skull."

"The heat."

"Yes. What were you asking about?"

"Oh! The Cove!"

"Cove?"

"Supposedly. Now, I'm no scientist."

"I remember your bio grade. You are correct in that assessment."

They row side by side for a bit, she's going back the way she came now. Why not? She hasn't spoken to anyone since that old booger-dick back at that gas station yelled at her about taking a box of zebra cakes. That was....... at least a year ago.

"What are you looking for?" she asks.

"The Cove."

"Oh."

"Mhm."

"What is that?"

"Where?"

"No.... The Cove. What is The Cove?"

"Oh! It's this place where supposedly some smart guy found cold air. Like there's a whole system of life underwater. It's like a giant cave filled with cool air."

"How is it not flooded?"

"I guess it's like holding a cup upside down in the bathtub."

"How do they breathe?"

"I don't know, do I look like an ichthyologist here, Denise? I guess plants.... or something."

"Oh."

"Yeah, they have like, cows or something down there to eat too. You gotta go through a cave up here on the surface."

"What about the carbon levels from the methane?"

"Again, I'm no scientist."

"Ok. What about where it is? It seems very illogical to me."

"Look around!" He waves his arms in a big circle. "The whole stinking place is illogical! The ice caps are almost gone. I've lost a hundred pounds. I eat fish that died and washed up."

"I can fish."

"Of course, you can fish."

"Look at us. Arguing like we haven't missed a beat."

"Yeah well, old habits, right? We dated for four years before you dumped my ass two days before our anniversary."

"I dumped you?"

"You said, and I quote 'this just isn't going to work'"

"I meant trying to have a serious relationship when the world was ending."

"Yeah, well."

"And then you avoided me for three weeks. Why didn't you skip that class anyway?"

"I don't know."

"Oh."

"Oh."

"You want me to catch you a fish and show you how to cook it?"

"Please."

They sat on the side of what used to be a cliff. Dangling their feet off the ledge into the water a foot below them. Eating the fish they cooked over a small fire. They looked like two kids at a pool party, eating lunch but dipping their toes into the water so they could still feel its coolness.

They talk about the little memories they have together. Denise eating too much at the Chinese restaurant but just having to have that bowl of strawberry ice cream, followed by Michael laughing at how pink her puke was as it hit the toilet later. They talk about the time Michaels Jeep had a flat tire and he swore up and down he didn't have a spare, only for Denise to show up and find the spare under the back seat. They talk distantly and sadly about their parents. They talk about how weird it is that they found each other here, at the end of the world. What are the odds? Denise tells Michael she thought the end was close and needed to be home for it. Michael tells Denise about how he's wasted his time travelling only to be told about the cove and how it is strangely enough in his hometown, no TV for years means news travels slow, especially about anything new. They sit and chat without paying attention to the sun. Before long it's lowered enough to cool the surface a little.

"We can share this mattress if you don't have anything." she says.

"I swear there isn't a spare in that kayak." he replies.

They sleep until the heat from the mattress wakes them up. They groggily go for a swim to wake up before paddling some more towards a destination Michael is confident exists, but Denise doubts. She's planning to enjoy her last few days or however long they have enjoying the company of a long-lost friend. Michael swears it's there; the mines have always been there. Who knew their salvation was so close all this time?

"Why were you going to propose?" she asks. "We all knew the planet was off course, the laps around the sun getting shorter and shorter."

"Well, I had already planned to do it on our five-year anniversary. I wasn't going to let that damn meteor ruin that too."

"Oh."

"Oh."

"When did communication get so hard?"

"Well, for me I'd say it was yesterday when we bumped into each other and I realized I hadn't talked to anyone in like, four years? Other than telling the pirates to leave me alone. Then here's the love of my life, just paddling along."

"Live of your life? Get real."

"It's true."

"Yeah ok, since when."

"Since the first time I saw you."

"When we got set up on a date?"

22

"No."

"Oh."

"It was at that ice cream place in 5th street."

"I don't remember the name."

"I was walking home from the library. I could see you through the window. It was raining, it was like a scene from a movie, and I was the lead actor. I looked in and saw you drinking a milkshake, you were laughing with friends and waving at another table. I knew then I was going to propose to you on our fifth anniversary. I had to run home and tell Ma."

"And what did she say?"

"She told me 'Michael, don't start going all dipshit on me. This isn't one of those teenage romance movies you've been watching lately. Ask the girl on a date first before you claim her as your own.'"

"Good advice, Ma."

They row in silence, both thinking about the Ma in question. Both thinking about their parents being somewhere under all of this water.

"The ice cream place closed a month later." he says.

"That little girl found a cockroach in her banana split." she says.

"That's disgusting."

"So is all this mushy stuff right now."

They laughed it off and splashed water at each other playfully. She taught him how to catch a fish that night before they slept.

The next morning, they were woken by the sound of two people yelling from far off.

"Come with us! The open sea is the only place to survive!" Yelled a voice.

"Why do they believe this shit?" she asks

"I think they misinterpreted a Bible verse or something. They think we're the one lost sheep and they're Jesus bring us back to the flock."

"I didn't want a real answer."

"Oh, it's because they really like having more people to talk to."

"Sadly, I think that's probably true too. Let's go before more than those two show up, I have a scar on my back that shows how little they like the answer 'no'"

They return to the subject of The Cove. Michael explains the entrance is an old mine. He knew the name of the particular entrance because he and his father hiked to it a few times when he was a kid.

"What if it floods that high?" she asks

"Again, I'm no scientist." He responds to that question and the next one about boiling water.

The day carries on much as the past two, joking and reminiscing. Denise making fun of Michael for never explaining where they were going, Michael making fun of Denise for blindly following him. She tells him she did that for almost half a decade already so what's a couple more days.

They reach a chunk of land, a path running along it to a hill and then onward. A sign that reads "The Cove" with an arrow pointing up the path.

"Oh my god I was right!" he shouts. "I was actually right!"

Together they pull the kayaks up far enough on the surface to feel confident they won't float away so they don't have to take the time to anchor them. They both walk up the path at a brisk pace before seeing another figure moving at a much brisker pace from their left.

"It's one of those damn Junkers." she says.

"Persistent little booger, isn't he?"

"Aren't all religious types?"

They move with haste up the path until they reach a wall made of rock. Footholds have been carved out of this face of rock allowing a person to climb straight up the twenty feet instead of walking around however far it would take.

They reach the wall and Denise starts climbing, she makes it two feet off the ground before the Junker is there yelling at them.

"Don't do it! There's a cave there! It's the gates of Hell! It swallows people whole and they're never seen again! Their souls left to burn for eternity!"

"What's the difference?" Asks Michael, keeping the man distracted so that Denise can finish her ascent. "I'm already burning right now, why not just skip the dying part and go right to the source."

"Ignorance. Ungodliness. Uncleanliness. Come with me. We can make you pure as the lamb." The Junker reaches out for Michael who grabs both of his arms in an attempt to block him. The Junker's right arm slips from Michael's grip, with the sweat building he's unable to regain control. The man punches him hard in the ear. Michael's vision crosses for a second and he quickly thinks he may have been better leaning his head forward instead of to the side. Another blow comes down and he feels consciousness slipping away. The Junker stands and grabs his feet and starts dragging him away.

He stops five feet into his journey when a sudden sharp pain erupts below the jawline on the right side of his head. He drops Michael's feet and turns slowly to look where the pain came from. His fingers find a warm substance flowing from the spot of the pain, and a large screw like piece of metal protruding from the wound. He falls over in shock and rolls down the path a few feet before settling against a tree.

"Is he dead?" Michael asks.

"I'm not a scientist. Let's go." Denise helps him back to his feet and they make their way up the rock wall. They walk for another mile, at least, and before them is a hole in the side of the mountain. A hole that has a wooden frame. A wooden frame that has the words "The Cove" painted on them.

"Happy anniversary." She says as they walk into the mouth of the cave clutching each other's hands.

NOTES:

David Bowie rullllzzzzz. This was a story I just had sort of hit me when listening to Bowie's track of the same name. Someone read this once and told me they did the research, and the Earth wouldn't flood enough to ever cover the appalachian mountains. To which I say they are an asshole who doesn't enjoy stories. What do I look like here? Some sort of scientist? I'm just making shit up. That's it. I mean, yah, I could check the science, but I don't want to and you shouldn't bother with it because this story was only like, what? Ten pages?

SMOKING
SECTION

@CSM1321

He feels the weight of another body slide into bed behind him; he feels a cold and scaly arm drape over its side, a hand rests on his chest.

He shakes the covers from his body and jumps out of bed as fast as a kid who thinks they're getting that drivable monster truck they wanted so badly.

He looks in the mirror facing his bed and sees it. Just like a bad horror movie trope he spins around and sees nothing.

Donovan slept in his car that night.

•

"No shit?" Asks Gary before he bites into his steak sub.

"No shit anywhere to be found. Except, maybe in my pants." says Donovan.

"What the hell did it look like?"

"It was grey. It didn't have any hair from what I could tell. It looked like a person in the face sort of, not anyone I've ever met before. I mean, I didn't get the best look at it, I thought I was dead."

"Yeah... wow... unbelievable, man."

Gary forces a small pile of chips into his mouth. *He's already forgotten what I just said*, thinks Donovan.

•

Donovan feels the weight crawl behind him again. This time he's determined to not be scared; maybe he can show this thing he is one with whom not to fuck and it will leave him alone.   He feels toes as long as fingers wrap around his foot and slide between his toes.

"NOPE!" He yells leaping from the bed.

Again, he looks in the mirror and this time all he sees is the thing's foot, four long toes that end in nails that looked as long and sharp as one of those knives from a late-night infomercial.

He commits the cardinal sin of the haunted house, he turns around.

Nothing.

He sleeps in his car again.

•

"That's literally the last thing you want to do." Donovan says to his girlfriend, Nina, on the car ride to her place.

"I've always wanted to stay in a haunted house. My aunt's house was haunted, it was so odd." says Nina.

"Yeah? You have weird grey people snuggling up behind you at all hours of the night?"

"Grey people? Is it maybe actually an alien?"

●

He slept at Nina's that night.

●

"You sure I can't stay?" Nina asks the next evening.

"Positive." says Donovan, "I have no idea if this thing is dangerous or what it is. Besides, I'm not letting anyone else spoon with you."

"You don't know what I do in my free time."

"I have a feeling there's a lot of food network competition shows involved."

"A LOT of Food Network competitive cooking shows. Jason loves them."

"Jason?"

"Mamoa."

"I think I can make an exception for Aquaman."

"More like Aquadaddy."

●

He leaves his phone on record while he sleeps.

Flour poured across the floor.

He wakes up at four in the morning hearing a deep scratch in wood.

He moves quickly to the light switch and fills the room with illumination.

He sees footprints in the flour; just as he planned to.

Four long scratches deep in the wood.

It looks as though the thing was pulled backwards by something.

●

"Ok, I'll listen to your little recording, but I still think you need to get ahold of my pastor, bro." says Gary.

"Snidutilos... te... singi... satinretea..." The voice on the recording is filled with gravel. It sounds like a child with a small housefire in its throat. The voice repeats over and over and over, increasing in volume until the sound of scratching and Donovan's footsteps fill the tiny phone speaker.

"Yeah, man. Call my pastor."

●

When he arrived home that night, he found a smiley face carved into the wall above his bed.

So, he called Gary's Pastor.

●

"Shouldn't there be some sort of explosion or something?" Donovan says.

"Nah," says the pastor, "that's movie stuff. You're good to go."

He slept just fine that night, and for sixteen days after.

•

An Email reads:
ATTENTION DESIGNERS!
Due to the increase in Covid-19 cases at Williamson Design Company and the recent government announcement of a two-week quarantine, we have decided to close in-person workdays. As of now, we plan to close the office indefinitely until it is determined to be completely safe to meet in person again. This may be two weeks; this may be two months. As always, thank you for all that all of you do, see you soon.

•

The first two weeks were ok. Donovan played a lot of video games, ate a ton of junk food. He always apologized to the Door dash workers for having to work in these conditions. He also apologized to the people who delivered his groceries. He didn't stop using either though. Somewhere in the middle of the third week he realized he was bored.

☐

He texts Nina.

Hey, Wanna come over tonight?
                    Are you an idiot, Donovan?
I'm not an idiot, NINA.
   You know I'm at mom's and you know she's
                    immune compromised.
I know, I'm just bored and sorta lonely.
         Awwwwwwwww poor thing. See if Gary
         wants to hang out or play games online.

      Gary was enjoying the time off; he
was taking advantage of all the extra time he
had with his wife and two sons.

●

      He went outside and took a walk
around his two acres; he couldn't remember
what interested him so much about the land
to buy this much of it. *Did I think I was going to
become a farmer? Did I truly believe I would ever
actually mow this lawn myself, or take long walks in
the woods? Fuck, this is so boring.*
      He spent the rest of the evening
checking his social media frantically.
      His ex-girlfriend from Freshman year
of high school had three kids and lived in
Texas now: good for her. Her mom passed
away last year, he felt himself frowning, she
was nice to him. Her father was still working,

the old workaholic, he hadn't met him once the whole time they were together.

His best friend from third grade seemed to have some sort of drug addiction problem. He was trying to sell everything he owned, including a used bedpan. A comment on one of his posts said, "Maybe get a job to fund ur needle addiciton, then u aint gota sail a used pisser." Sure, that would help the blister caused by the burn, but it wouldn't heal the burn.

His aunt was cooking again; that's so good. She loved cooking, why had she ever stopped? A failing restaurant isn't any reason to give up on something you love doing.

His ex from junior year was running some sort of pyramid scheme, or maybe it was a fake profile using her name and photo.

•

He slept restlessly that night.

•

He called his parents the next morning, hoping he could go stay with them for a bit or they would come to his house. His mom told him that there would be no room. His Brother and his sister-in-law were staying with their daughter. She explained that being a retired teacher would be a big help for her granddaughter's homeschooling.

36

He kicked around for six hours, ordered two subs from Subway so he didn't have to order food again tomorrow.

•

He slept with the weight of boredom and loneliness, holding his eyes open and making every position mildly uncomfortable.

•

He realized his error of ordering food in advance. Today he wouldn't even get to have the through a closed-door convo with the delivery person. He called Gary's pastor that evening and was reassured he couldn't accidentally bring back the demonic entity just by simply being lonely.

"Christ," says the pastor, uncharacteristically taking the lord's name in vain, "You couldn't even bring that thing back if you tried."

•

That night he fell asleep thinking about how even a scaly and arctic embrace would be better than the solitude he was stuck in.

•

He ordered food twice the next day. The first person was a woman, he didn't want to invite her in because that seemed pretty sketch and no matter how lonely he was, he didn't want to scare anyone.

He put the pizza she delivered in the fridge and immediately ordered another.

The guy knocked on his door and set the pizza on the table beside that was being used for deliveries.

He opened the door and yelled "HEY!" at the guy before he got in his car.

"Hey, what's up? Pizzas on the table."

"Thanks, you got a break coming up or anything?"

"We're pretty slammed. Kind of in a hurry."

"You sure you can't spare a few minutes to come in and have a slice or two?"

"No way, boss says we can't go in anywhere. Too risky with, you know, everything going on."

"What if I just opened a window and you sat on the porch?"

"Still too risky for me, my man. I get you; I get lonely too, I only see people at work and my boyfriend. It's rough for sure!"

"Yeah... hey, have a good day, thanks for the food."

"You too! Hang in there, dude. We're gonna all get through this stronger."

Pizza guy is full of shit, he thought as he watched Home Improvement re-runs through the natural underwater filter his tears were putting on life.

•

Hey, his boss... now there's an idea! He thought before grabbing his phone and asking his boss if they could have a video chat tomorrow about something.

•

"What do you mean?" asks the face on his phone screen.

"I don't know if the design for that sign I sent will work."

"The client loved it. They can't wait until all of this is over so they can pick it up."

"Oh, ok, that's great."

"Yep, so no worries. Enjoy your time at home. Anything else?"

"Yeah, actually..."

"Shoot."

"How is... everything?"

"Everything?"

"Yeah... like life... and stuff."

"Are you ok, Donovan?"

"Yeah, just a little lonely."

"I understand, the only people I've seen in weeks are my wife, our son and his wife, their three kids. It gets pretty bad. Hang

39

in there, we're gonna get through this and
come out as better people."

•

My boss is full of shit. He thought as he
tried to shut his eyes over the tap of water
that seemingly opened.

•

He spent the next day trying all
manner of stupidity. He jumped off the couch
pretending it was an airplane and the blanket
he held behind him was a parachute. He
mixed every condiment in his fridge and
tasted it; he cleaned up the puke. He lay on
the ground screaming out in agony as the
pizza he ordered yesterday was cooking in the
oven. He cried out in agony, his boredom and
loneliness taking on a physical form. It had
become a wound that was so deep it made his
heart feel like it was made of bone and had a
hundred fractures in it.

•

Eventually he went to bed.
He fell asleep looking at articles about
summoning a demon.

•

The rituals of the next day proved fruitless in summoning a demon but did keep his mind occupied for a few hours. The pentagram he drew on the small chalkboard he had on his fridge didn't catch fire. The water he filled the sink with didn't bubble when he spoke the incantations over it. He didn't try to sacrifice an animal; he caught a worm in his yard but couldn't bring himself to purposely kill it. As he let the worm go in his yard, he watched it wiggle away through blades of grass, on its way to its own family and people.

"Go on, you little thing. Go see your people. We don't all have to be alone." He sat on the ground and felt that deep pain again and began crying.

He spent the rest of the evening sobbing while the toolman grunted away on a Home Improvement re-run he had already watched.

●

He feels the weight of another body slide into bed behind him; he feels a cold and scaly arm drape over its side, a hand rests on his chest.

He smiles and sleeps peacefully.

NOTES:

The pandemic has really sucked, yeah? Not only do we have to deal with a bunch off assholes refusing to wear a piece of cloth that could potentially save lives, but now we have to deal with a virus that can kill us AND lonliness. I think most of us have experienced the dread of another day without human interaction at least once these past few years. I've gotten so lonely that I wished I had a ghost to talk to; so, here's this story. Also, there was a local mega church pastor trying to run for school board in my locale because he said wearing masks was against his religious beliefs. What an asshole. More on assholes like him in the next story.

PRETTY PENNY THE PISSED-OFF POLTERGEIST VS. THE Q'ANON ARMY

"He was screaming at me about how our baby wasn't his, how I cheated on him with a liberal so I could sacrifice the baby to Tom Hanks"
-Anita Riddle
Taken from "Surviving a Modern-Day Cult- First-Hand Accounts of Q'Anon Survivors" by Reid Cadle

•

Penny was gazing off into the distance, watching people come and go, hoping one would come into the building built on her unmarked grave. "Jesus H. Christ, I have never believed in you, but if you would just let one of these schmucks walk in here, I will owe you big big." She spoke to an empty room.

This building has been Penny's home for nearly fifty years; killed in 1973 by the police and buried right on the spot the bullet landed after passing through her skull. A killing spree that lasted close to four years ended with one single bullet smashing its way through the bone above her right eye, through the mush of her brain, and somehow back out of her head before plopping on the ground no more than ten feet behind her body. As she stumbled and fell on the ground, she rolled her head to the side and could see the bullet beside her, taunting her, saying "Great job

45

killing all those people! Sorry I had to barge in and end it before you could hit forty-five."

The bullet wasn't the only thing that mocked her that day. The police stood over her lifeless body, and she found herself standing up beside them looking down at her dead body. What an unpleasant experience that was, seeing her own brain matter spread out across the dry grass-covered field.

"We should bury her here." Said one of the three officers that chased her into this open field. "They're building that warehouse here in a month, no one will ever know where she is. That way we won't have any crazies trying to worship Satan or some such manner of bullshit on her grave."

To prevent crazies from worshipping Satan or some such manner of bullshit on the final resting place of Pretty Penny, they did just that. She was buried deep in the Earth and covered under cold, hard cement.

She looked out the window and reminisced about that day, watching people go in and out of the other buildings built around her tomb. People had stopped coming in way back in 1985 when she pushed a warehouse worker's ladder over and sent him falling twelve feet to the unforgiving ground. Luckily for him, his head took most of the fall and he was dead instantly. Stories of the building being haunted would keep any buyer away from the place for decades, newer buildings popping up all around this old one didn't help either.

She was rubbing her ghostly stomach and thinking about how her stomach should be rumbling for the nourishment of the kill like it was a plate of pancakes when a smell hit her nose. The smell was of sour bacon and month-old cigarette smoke. She pokes her head out over the railing of the second floor. She gazes down to the empty factory floor and sees two men talking. One waving his arms around in a suit and tie, clearly trying to sell the building; the other in a pair of blue jeans, a black shirt with the face of Jesus on it (not actual Jesus, but the surfer bro Jesus everyone has come to know), and a red ball cap with white lettering that read "Make America Great Again." *Whatever the fuck that means*, Penny thinks, *I've been reading newspapers when they blow in here and phone screens of passersby, let me say this place just isn't great and hasn't been great.* She also thinks she may be a little biased being as how she kills people just for the fun of killing something. *Probably a pretty pessimistic mindset there,* she thinks.

"I only need the place for one day!" says the man in the cap.

"That's still the price, I'm sorry." says the suit man.

"Well, at least if I do it through my church, I won't have to pay taxes. So, that helps… yeah, ok, I'll do it."

"Great! I'll meet you here Saturday."

They continue talking on the way out of the building. At the same time, a grin crosses Penny's face.

•

"I told my parents I didn't agree with a lot of Trump's rhetoric, it was honestly disgusting. I told them I was voting Biden and I was homeless in the next half of an hour."

-Peter Oliver

Taken from "Surviving a Modern-Day Cult- First-Hand Accounts of Q'Anon Survivors" by Reid Cadle

•

If the smell was bad before, it was triple that now. Every single one of these people smelled like spoiled bacon and old cigarettes. Some of them had the added bonus of not showering in a week. She stared at all the booths spread out on the floor, trying to figure out how she could even smell.

Can ghosts smell? Sure, why not, better torture me some more, she thinks to herself.

She decides to brave the smell and get a closer look, but she doesn't want to accidentally materialize in the middle of all of that and cause a panic. She makes herself the smallest particle of matter and drops through the floor into the women's restroom. She hears a voice in a stall, "Listen, I'm doing this for you and the kids! If someone doesn't

48

stand up to the left's child-eating-human-trafficking-Muslim-loving ways, then it really could be our kids in the back of a van forced to wear a hijab and pray to Allah before being sold to Biden or Harris as a sacrifice or sex toy! … He hung up on me!"

A phone comes sliding across the floor and hits the wall. Penny hovers above the woman in the stall and sees her buttoning her jeans. She concentrates on the possession; she hasn't done this in way too long.

The woman's brain barely puts up a fight, she slides right into the controls as easy as hot butter into a colon. She steps out of the stall and checks herself out in the mirror. She has long blonde hair tied into a ponytail fed through the back of the same red hat that the man was wearing, a t-shirt that says, "Trump can grab me by the pussy!", and a face covered in a bit too much foundation. She does a little spin and is impressed, the woman has kept herself in a lot better shape than most of the people she's seen today, she doesn't even smell bad.

As soon as she leaves the bathroom the decent smell is overcome by that same old nastiness she smelt earlier.

"Jesus Christ." She says when it hits her new nasal passages.

"Do you need someone to pray with?" Says a small woman sitting in a folding chair beside the bathroom door.

"No, I'm good… God is good and all that."

"Amen, sister. He is!"

She walks into the fray of people, seeing things she can't believe people would advertise.

She chats with a man at a booth selling bumper stickers and shirts that say, "Build that wall!" with a depiction of sweaty brown people in sombreros falling from a massive concrete wall.

"What does this mean?" she asks.

"You know what it means. Keep the Mexicans from taking over our nation!"

"Oh, yeah, I know what it is. Sure, damn Mexicans. One of them delivered a pizza to my house the other day and I about puked."

"You didn't eat it did you?"

"Of course not! I can't eat! I don't believe people are climbing a wall though. Some people have other ways of coming to America seeking immigration to make their lives better, like flying."

"What in the libtard-fuck did you say? They ain't all got helicopters, lady. What's all this immigration shit? You pulling my leg?"

"…Sure …I guess …We weren't just joking around?"

"You better have been joking around saying immigration is a good thing! Keep Americans in American jobs!"

She nods and walks away. *Holy shit,* she thinks, *I'm a pretty terrible awful person, but that guy can't seriously be that racist.*

She paused at another booth with a sign advertising gay marriage as the worst sin, one that makes God sick.

"Aren't all sins supposed to be the same?" She asks the woman and man behind the table.

"Except for when two men fornicate!" Says the man with a disgusted look on his face.

"What about two women? I bet you love that though."

The woman glares at him when he takes a millisecond too long to say "No… That's pretty gross too."

Sure, she thinks, probably have a ton of it saved in a shoebox under the bed, or on these new phones I see everyone with outside.

The next place she stops is a pro-life booth. She doesn't even engage in conversation; she just picks up a tiny plastic baby fetus and bites the head off it. She stares into the two women behind the table's eyes as she spits it out and does the same to another. She hears loud music booming up ahead and heads toward it.

She finds herself standing behind a crowd gathered in front of a stage. The man who was here days ago walks onto the stage wearing the same outfit with the addition of a button-up flannel shirt.

"Thank you for joining me here today, Folks!" He says, grabbing the microphone. "I hope you're all enjoying your day and getting the necessary information to stop the rise of the evil left!"

The crowd cheers, all except for a boy of about twelve standing off to the side of the stage with a woman who looks almost identical to the one she's possessed.

"My son, Reid." Says the man motioning over to the boy and woman. "He said to me 'Dad, I don't want to go to your church thing. I want to go to the Meghan Trainor concert.' Let me tell you, my friends, I was so disgusted with myself. I thought I had done a good job raising this young man up in the image God wanted for a young man. Now he's wanting to go watch this… harlot, for lack of better terms, dance around in skimpy outfits? I looked her up, she's part of the liberal elitist. She promotes that nasty thing called 'body positivity' that's so hot right now, the same with 'feminism' and 'l g t b h whatever!'"

The crowd cheers again and Penny can't help but notice the irony in these folks being mad about body positivity when most of them aren't exactly supermodels.

"I explained to him, no, no we aren't going to watch her turn young men of God into slaves of Satan before our very eyes! She probably runs a child trafficking ring! These people need sustenance from the blood of children to stay as young as they are! Look at Tom Hanks! He hasn't aged in a day!"

What the hell do you all have against Tom Hanks? she thinks to herself remembering one of the last times she watched a movie was when the town played "BIG" on a screen in the park she could see from the roof. Sure, she wanted to kill the guy, but she kind of wants to kill everyone, he at least made her laugh.

The speech rambles on for another five minutes about the craziest shit she's heard: politicians killing rivals, the Clintons involved in a child sex ring, and all manner of celebrities pushing what the man called "the evil left agenda."

"How about this 'BLM, Black Lives Matter' movement?" He asks a disgruntled crowd. "BLM… Black Lives Matter? More like belt loops matter!" He says as the crowd cheers.

"Alright! Alright! I can't take it anymore!" Penny yells as the crowd dies down. She walks toward the stage in anger "The crazy eating babies' stuff, that was interesting and downright funny. Racism? NOPE! Not going to happen. I hope y'all are paying taxes too. Churches don't get taxed so they can stay out of politics, right?" The crowd parts for her like she is Moses slamming her staff down in the Red Sea.

She stands at the foot of the stage as the man prepares to say something to her. Neither gets the chance to speak because a woman in the back yells "That's her! That's the she-devil who bit the heads off our babies!" The crowd turns toward her with hate in their eyes. She sends her spirit out to lock all the doors in the building so no one can leave.

She looks up into the man's eyes and says "Ignore my first question, I know the answer. What's your name?"

"Dennis Cadle, a man of God." he replies.

"Nice to meet you, Dennis. My name is Andrea Landall, or Pretty Penny as you probably recognize. Hang out here for a bit, it looks like I have some things to take care of, but then you and I are going to have a chat, ok?"

•

"The cops didn't even try to hide how they were helping those people. We were just visiting D.C., my wife and I were showing the kids all the landmarks when our son, Tyler, asked 'Daddy, isn't that flag mean to us?' And pointed to a confederate flag heading up the steps of the capital. I picked him up with tears in

54

my eyes and said "Yeah, it is. I'm sorry."
And held him as close to me as I could."

-Todd Woods

Taken from "Surviving a Modern-Day Cult- First-
Hand Accounts of Q'Anon Survivors" by Reid
Cadle

•

"Anyone who doesn't want to get
spread across this floor like the nasty shit-
stains you are, please make your way to the
second floor and I will allow you to leave after
all this." Penny yells. No one moves, they only
appear to get angrier. A man walks forward
and puts his hand on her right shoulder, she
grabs the hand and jerks it hard ripping it
from the shoulder. She spins around and hits
him on the head with the limb, splitting his
skull open.

The crowd surges and moves toward
her. She punches a man through the stomach
and grabs his intestine then runs a loop
around the crowd in her spectral form before
re-entering her host. She uses her spectral
power and squeezes the organs crunching the
people in this devilish lasso together until they
can't move.

The rest of the crowd backs off from
this gory spectacle in a sort of surrender. *Too
late for that,* she thinks. She levitates knives,
swords, and axes from a booth and sends
them shooting through the crowd toward her
new project. They pierce through other

members of the crowd everywhere, blood shooting into the air like it's from a fire hose, the sounds of metal slicing through bone, and the screams and groans right before death. The weapons hover around the group trapped in the intestine and move quickly severing all their legs. The group drops down far enough that the intestine is flat on the ground. She walks to the side and reaches out to a man facing away from her, she bends him back hearing his spine snap until he's lying flat on the ground. She does this to the next four people and steps back making the intestine squeeze harder on the group. Bones begin to crack and crunch; blood covers them all.

"How about this for a red hat!" She shouts. "You all seem to love them so much that I thought I'd make my own!"

She doesn't get the chance to finish that sentence as a bullet passes through her skull and out of her eye socket. The body she's using falls forward and the ghostly figure of Penny stands staring down at it.

"Damnit!" she sighs. "Not again! Same damn way too!" She turns to see Dennis holding the gun. She hears the survivors screaming and moaning behind her trying to escape. Dennis fires another round at Penny, it passes through her, and she sends it flying through the heads of all the survivors except Dennis and his little family.

She moves fast and throws Dennis to the ground in front of his wife and son.

"You're worse at pretending to be a human than I ever was." she says. "You've used words to convince all of these people to use hate as a weapon against smaller, less fortunate groups of people. Those people already deal with enough shit, that's why I never, NEVER killed based on appearance. I hate people as a whole. I hate what they do to one another, I hate what they do to our planet, and most importantly; I hate people like you. I made a career out of killing the slugs of the

Earth like you; fascists, religious nut jobs, the users and abusers of society. I guess no one ever realized that did they? Do you know why they called me Pretty Penny, Dennis?"

"… Please let us go." He begs.

"You're going to die, Dennis. I really believe that, but I haven't gotten that far yet. I don't believe your son or wife will, but again, not quite there yet. Answer my question. Do you know why I was called Pretty Penny?"

"Yes… because everywhere you killed, there was so much blood it filled men's sinuses, they said finding one of your victims made it seem like their mouths were filled with pennies."

"You can almost chew the taste of blood in here, can't you? What about the pretty part?"

"I guess because you're a woman."

"Right. If it's a woman, she has to be 'baby' or 'honey' or 'pretty' some form of bullshit, right? Here's what I think. Hey, Reid, what's your mom's name?"

"Uhhhhh…" he says through his teeth that have been clenched tightly in fear. "I think it's Melinda?" He looks up at his mother who nods slowly.

"Nice to meet you both! Reid, Melinda, what do you think I should do here? This is your chance to speak."

Melinda steps forward and punches Dennis in the face.

"Fuck you!" She yells in his face. "I'm so tired of being your trophy! Do you know how annoying it is to have to wear these outfits? To do my makeup like this every day? To see all these other men look at me like I'm a great hunk of meat you scored? Of course not. You're too busy telling my son how the white males of America are better than everyone else. I don't even believe in this shit! I voted for Obama twice and I'm so happy Biden won! I pray every day to gain the courage to take Reid and leave you. I've let you hold power over us way too long and now this nice… ghost?"

Penny shrugs.

"Now she's giving me a chance for freedom and I'm taking it."

"You voted for…. A Muslim… that's not Christian…" He mumbles in shock.

"Obama has been a member of the same Christian church for decades! Get your head out of your ass and learn some facts before you come up on these stages ruining people's lives!" She yells while hitting him three more times.

"Reid…" he says. "Is this how you feel too?"

"I did really want to go see Meghan Trainor." He says before turning his face into his mother's bosom crying.

"I think that about settles it." says Penny.

Dennis watches as Reid and Melinda exit out of a side door without looking back at him. He looks up at Penny and realizes he's staring into the eyes of a worse hell than any he's preached about.

•

"I'll never forget that day. My dad went crazy. He started shooting people and reloading so fast that I swear to you he had to be in the marines or something. My mother punched him so much he fell unconscious, I guess when he woke up and we were gone, he saw what he did, that was when he killed himself and set the building on fire. I just hope his soul is trapped in that spot with the ghosts of everyone he killed. The best justice that I

can imagine is having to face all of those angry spirits for eternity."

Reid Cadle

Taken from "Surviving a Modern-Day Cult- First-Hand Accounts of Q'Anon Survivors" by Reid Cadle

NOTES:
THESE PEOPLE RULZZZZZ
Meghan Trainor

THESE PEOPLE ARE ASSHOLES
Racists
Xenophobes
Sexists
Homophobes
Transphobes
Pro-life dipshits
Christians who have clearly never read The Bible
The NRA
K THX!

THE BODY IS A TEMPLE

@CGM1321

Therefore I tell you, do not worry about your life, what you will eat or drink; or about your body, what you will wear. Is not life more than food, and the body more than clothes?
Matthew 6:25

●

A cotton swab dips into a jar filled with the blood of a newborn... SUPPOSEDLY a newborn, anyway. The last jar of "Blood of a Newborn" Dr. Uriah Devers bought turned out to be just red Kool-aid packaged up in an elaborately designed canning jar.

"Uhhhhhh... that's like, only supposed to be a Halloween decoration, my man." Said the seller on eBay. Fucking loser, Uriah thinks, another one of these fly-by-nighters who thinks wearing some shirt with an indecipherable band name on it is the key to Satanism.

Records aren't evil, Joe.

As he draws the pentagram upon his newest subject's stomach he thinks back to his last attempts; Sloth was ripped down the middle by an unseen force, leaving a mess of all his insides on the ground, Pride's skin began to boil and pop like the skin of a pig in hot oil, and Lust... poor Lust... her belly

63

button opened up and sprayed all of her insides out like a high-powered firehose. It took Uriah two weeks of two showers a day to finally get all the bits of Lust off his body; even now he still finds a spot of blood or pebble sized bit of bone he missed.

This had to be the one. Gluttony had to be it. To Uriah the issue had to be size, it had become clear the bodies of the previous three subjects couldn't contain the massive presence of The Dark Lord within their frames. Gluttony had to be it. This man was large enough for Uriah to crawl inside his belly, so surely that would be enough room for Satan?

He finishes with the blood and makes his way into the other room. He stands in a control room behind a glass window. In front of the window is a room painted red with the symbols associated with a summoning painted over every inch of the wall. In the middle of the room lays a naked man, a pentagram drawn upon his stomach, an inverted cross placed in each of his spread hands. The only thing that formerly the man's nakedness was the small hospital gown he wore before taking "an experimental weight loss" supplement that was actually a heavy tranquilizer.

The man lays in the room surrounded by melting candles, the home of his body waiting for a new resident.

One of Uriah's assistants makes eye contact hoping his mental plea to get started is heard. Uriah nods and pushes a lever forward playing a thousand voices at once in the room. The voices are every known recording of demons speaking, as well as every possible chant to summon Satan.

"Weight loss treatment…" he chuckles to himself. "You must be fat AND dumb, my friend." He says looking at the man in the other room.

"Hey, now. There's just flat out no reason to insult the guy's physical appearance." says a voice behind him. Uriah turns around to find the three assistants he had in the room with him have seemingly melted together into a mass of blood-soaked skin and protruding bones. A head sits atop the mass, the face unrecognizable. The mouth again opens and speaks, "Your bonkers you know? This whole operation is shady as shit. I've been kind of fucking with you here and there, ripping people up, making you think you did something wrong. You didn't, I've been here the whole time."

"Satan?" asks Uriah under his breath.

"Say it with your full chest, you silly bastard! You wanted me, you got me! Why the long face? Is it because I'm supposed to be in THAT room in THAT nice man on the floor? You thought you had me, didn't you?"

"I… uh… well…"

"You... uh... well... well you made a fool of yourself, as I expected. I was kind of just kicking around waiting for another person to make into Jell-O, but I wasn't keen on the insults you were hurling at the guy you expected me to jump into. Thought I'd hop in there and you'd have me trapped in your little room and I'd do whatever you asked, right? RIIIGHHHHTTTTT? Well, good doctor, we're gonna have us some fun tonight. Can you say 'whoops-a-daisy?'"

"…. Whoops-a-daisy?"

"Amen."

•

Kerry Young woke up in a jolt when he felt something burning a hole in his nipple. He sat up in pain and shock only to find it was melted candle wax that had already hardened.

"Little nipple shell." He said out loud to himself half a second before his brain asked "Why am I naked? Why is there a star on my stomach? How did that wax drip on me?" He jumped up in a hurry and looked around the dark room.

"I should have known!" He yells as he smacks his hand into the front of his face. "This is why I don't try these things. One minute it's a pill, the next it's a parasitic worm, then all of a sudden you wake up as a

66

ritualistic sacrifice to Satan. SON OF A BITCH MUST PAY!" He storms over to the only door in the room and finds it to be perfectly flat. No doorknob, no handle, nothing. He sees the mirror at the front of the room and walks over so he's in front of it. "I'm naked and pissed!" he yells. "I can't get out of here, I can't find any clothes because it's dark, turn on the lights. Turn! On! The! Lights!"

The lights do not come on.

"Let there be light!"

There was no light.

"Lacarnum Inflamari!"

Nothing caught fire except J.K. Rowling's career after exposing herself as a giant asshole.

"Hermione, you did me wrong here. That spell didn't work."

He walks around the room feeling the wall and eventually stands on the hospital gown they had him put on. He slides it back down onto his body.

He finds the page ripped from a People magazine Lucy gave him in the pocket. He thinks back to sitting in the waiting room explaining to another man that he didn't care to lose weight, he just wanted the extra cash the experiment was offering.

●

"You're not here to lose weight?" The man said.

"Nope. Life is very simple, I can weigh one-fifty and not eat Parmesan Bread Bites from Domino's and have to cut into my free time to exercise, or I can eat Parmesan Bread Bites from Domino's and have all the free time I could possibly want."

"So… Why come then?"

"They're offering a thousand bucks to take a single pill and stay here for ten hours. I can take two weeks off work with that kind of cash. Go on a little trippy-trip or something with it, you know what I mean?"

"Shrooms?"

"No, I don't really like 'em."

"You said 'trippy-trip' so I thought you meant like… psychedelics."

"Trippy-trip? It's a vacation."

"A vacation on $1000?"

"I'm easy."

"I'm not."

"Good for you."

"Good for me."

The man was as irritating as a rock caught in the tread of a shoe. Kerry got up and went and sat by a woman across the room who was reading an issue of People magazine. Her dark brown hair running down the edges of her face like the frame around some really fancy piece of art in some really fancy museum.

"I think Ben and Jennifer are back together again." she said.

"Oh, that's good." Kerry said, not knowing what the Hell she was going on about.

"Do you think it'll last this time?"

"With Ben? Nah, he's an asshole."

"You don't know who I'm talking about do you?"

"I thought you had me confused with someone you know; I was going to play along so I could get some gossip about strangers."

"You still are."

"I guess so."

"Ben Affleck and Jennifer Lopez."

"Wasn't he Super, man?"

"Batman."

"I know he played Batman, it's a joke. Like isn't he super, comma, Man?"

"I'm not a man."

"Definitely not."

"And it's not as funny because he wasn't Superman or super, man."

"Reckon I'll go introduce my head to my ass in the bathroom now."

They both share an awkward laugh before the woman says "Lucy Garret."

"Who'd she get back together with?" Kerry asks.

"No one, she was dating a guy a while ago, but it didn't work out."

"Who was he?"

"Just a guy whose life was going in a different direction than mine."

"Kerry Young."

"No, his name was James."

"Maybe Lucy Garret and Kerry Young could go on a sort of date. Someone should set them up. I think Kerry would ask if he didn't think it was too weird to ask Lucy after they had only met five minutes ago in a clinic for an experimental drug."

"I think that usually Lucy would be pretty annoyed about that quick of an approach, but she knows Kerry is about to make $1000 and traditional gender roles would imply he would be buying dinner for Lucy with it."

"Traditional gender roles also would say Lucy just agreed because she is a woman, and women only care about money."

"I built my own house."

"I couldn't possibly care less about cars."

"A couple of weirdos."

"Oh, they're a couple now?"

"That man is staring at us."

Kerry looks over to the man he was sitting with before and as sure as a dog will kick up the grass to cover its poop, the man frantically picks up a magazine and buries his face in it.

"Lucy Garret." says a woman holding a door open.

"Looks like I'm first. If you decide to leave before they call you up, here's my number." She says writing it on a page in the magazine. "I'm about to make $1000 so dinner can be on me, I'll be your sugar mama."

"A couple of weirdos."

"I think so."

•

He stands in the dark room looking at the picture of Ben and Jen, a phone number written across Jen's forehead.

He stops reminiscing and puts the number back in the pocket when he hears the door of the red room make a loud click.

It swings open and a figure is standing in the doorway.

"Kerry Young." says the same woman who took him from reception area to the small room, only this time her voice sounds like a broken lawnmower.

Light from the hallway illuminates her silhouette showing the handles of a pair of scissors sticking from her head. She reaches up and grabs the handle, pulling the scissors from her skull. The metal blades pulling up clumps of blood-soaked hair and sliced brain matter into the atmosphere.

"I really don't need that $1000 this bad." Says Kerry while the woman runs at him. He feels her hit him hard in his stomach and he falls reaching for her hand holding the scissors. "Snip snip! Now everyone's gonna think your hip!" She yells in his face, teeth slamming together hard enough to shatter them. He feels a rainfall of broken teeth and blood coat his face. His feet find traction on the cold linoleum floor, and he manages to twist his body and roll over with the woman. He sits on top of her trying to take the scissors from her hand. She breaks free of his grip and lashes out slamming them closed on the tip of his thumb. The pain sends him into an unexpected rage, and he slams his fist down into her face. She looks dazed and rolls her head back onto the floor.

"Shit! I'm sorry, you nipped off the end of my thumb! I just reacted the same way-"he's cut off by the scissors snipping so close to his ear lobe they manage to trim the tiny hairs lining it. He jumps backwards avoiding another snip at his nose.

His hand hits one of the bowls the candles sit in. He grabs it and throws it at her sending hot max and an open flame careening into her face. She grabs her eyes and stumbles around before slipping on some of her own blood and falling. The back of her head slams hard on the ground, her hair landing in one of the other candles and catching fire.

"Your hair!" Kerry shouts watching as her entire head is engulfed in flames. He runs to the doorway to escape the world's worst smelling Jack-o-lantern. He looks out into the hallway in both directions. He sees a sign that reads "Women A-H" with an arrow pointing to the left.

"I'll be damned if she's getting out of buying me dinner that easily." He says as he follows the arrow.

•

Kerry opens the first door he comes to in an underlit hallway. "Lucy? Are you here by any chance? This whole place has some pretty stereotypical hospital in a horror movie vibes going on and I'd kind of like to just leave." he says into the room. Above him a light flickers, he can see a sheet hanging from the ceiling separating the beds. The sheet is soaked in blood. "See what I mean." He says and walks toward the sheet with a sigh. He pulls it back and sees a man lying on the bed. His head has been placed inside his stomach. It looks like a bird's nest for sadistic swans; *Do swans even have nests?* He thinks.

The eyes open and the head begins to rise up out of the stomach. Intestines spill over the side of the bed propelling the head across the floor like an octopus. "ABSOLUTELY FUCKING NOT!" He shouts before kicking the head between the eyes. It rolls across the floor and hits a cabinet.

"Goal!" Yells the head as it twists its bloody tentacles up around the handles and nozzle of the sink built above. It twists the hot water faucet on and flicks an arm through the stream sending boiling hot water spotting all over Kerry's body. Kerry feels like he's being stung by a whole hive of wasps. He doesn't hesitate to think about the smell the creature creates when it burns itself. He hides behind the sheet and takes a deep breath, planning to charge the door as fast as he can. He peeks around the sheet and sees the demon octopus sucking the boiling hot water up into one of the intestines, he doesn't think about his escape anymore and takes off full sprint. He can hear the water spraying behind him and burning everything it touches. He slides back into the hallway and falls on the boiling water. He starts screaming as he lands in the puddle.

It's cold.

He thinks about how lucky he has to be that water heated up by some Hell-Octopus doesn't stay hot for too long, until he sees it's blood he's fallen in and standing above him is a skinless woman.

"How is all of that staying together?" He says without thought.

"Sort of like muscle I guess?" she says.

"Muscle huh? Your organs are just there. And you're bleeding like Niagara Falls."

"I'm not standing here trying to have a science lesson with you."

"Oh… what is it you're standing here for then?"

"I was going to go ahead and kill you."

"That's a bit of a problem for me. I sort of have a schedule conflict with that. I met a really pretty girl and she said she'd go on a date with me."

"Oh, how sweet. Would next Friday be better for you?"

"Hmmm, I think I'm scheduled for a haircut that day."

"You may have to reschedule."

The woman peels back layers of fleshy muscle and grabs one of her rib bones. She doesn't make a noise as she breaks it off and charges at Kerry. Kerry backs up on his hands, sliding his backside across the floor in a crawl. He burns his hand when he places it in the water coming from the room he just escaped. He rolls to the side and watches as the woman runs into the room. Her feet go out from under her, and she lands in the boiling hot water while the Hell-Demon-Octopus-Bastard sprays her down with more water. The incident is reminiscent of a cooking show and America's Funniest Home Videos all at the same time.

"Kerry?" He hears a voice down the hall. He looks and sees Lucy standing there covered in blood. He hurries over to her only to feel a hard thunk on the top of his head when he reaches her and the floor hitting his back.

"Are you normal? Or are you going to start eating your toes and spitting the bones at me like a machine gun?" Lucy says standings over him holding a chunk of wood.

"Where did you get a chunk of wood like that?" Kerry asks.

"It's like an axe handle that got cut in half, right?"

"Yeah, it really packs a wallop"

"Sorry."

"You're fine. You never can be too sure around here all of a sudden. Still, I wish you would have asked first."

"I asked the last guy."

"Yeah?"

"He ate his toes."

"He may have just been hungry though."

Lucy sighs and helps Kerry up.

A set of double doors at the end of the hall flies open. The rest of the hospital is engulfed in darkness. They can hear whispers of tortured souls and screams of pain floating through the air like a fog.

Above the doors, the exit sign lights up and continues to brighten until it explodes.

A dark red glow emits from the room behind the doors.

"Not very subtle, is it?" says Lucy

"Nope. Pretty heavy handed." Kerry says as they walk toward the doorway.

●

"Well, well, well… if it isn't the consequences of my own actions." says Dr. Uriah Devers. He stands with his back to Kerry and Lucy as they walk into the waiting room. "He said if I can get rid of all of my test subjects, he would allow me a sliver of the power I tried to steal. He's pretty understanding, really."

"…Huh?" says Lucy.

"It's like he started the whole evil monologue thing in the middle." says Kerry.

"Yeah, I feel like I've missed something?"

"It's a lot like when I watch a sequel without seeing the original?"

"You do that?"

"I have before. You see, like, Friday the 13Th Part 6 and assume they've had six shots at this, so surely the new is the bes-"

"ALRIGHT! JESUS H CHRIST! Can you shut the fuck up now?" says Dr. Devers.

"Sorry, Dr Devers." says Kerry.

"Just call me Uriah." says Uriah.

"That's kind of you, I wasn't aware we were on first name basis."

"I just don't really care about all the fluff and ego of a title. It's fine really."

"Could you turn around? It's hard having this conversation with you not facing us."

Uriah sighs and says "Well, I did have a whole thing planned out, then the big reveal. You sort of ruined that though."

"Sorry, Uriah."

"It's ok. You're right, I didn't think it through. I assumed you had as much information about the scenario as I did."

"That's understandable."

Uriah sighs again and turns around.

"FUCK!" Yells Kerry taking a step back.

"HOLY KOALA ORDERING A DRINK AT APPLEBEES!" yells Lucy.

Standing before them is the shape of a man, the shape is made from a million blood-soaked organs moving like snakes inside his skeleton. Each organ has a small human face on one end and a pair of pincers on the other.

"HA! Behold what my master has given me!" Shouts a very prideful Uriah.

"Worms?" asks Kerry.

"Huh? No… these are the souls of the Damned. I can use them like arms." Explains a saddened Uriah.

"They sure look like worms." says Lucy.

"This isn't shaping out to be anything like I thought it would."

"What's that they say about the best laid plans?"

"Too true. I just wish sometimes things would work out a little more the way I planned; you know?"

"I understand. I'm a planner, myself. I don't really care for spontaneity."

"Oh my God! Are we the same person?"

"Maybe!"

"Now I feel kind of bad."

"I'm sure you don't have any reason to."

"Well… like I said before… I kinda tried to hold Satan hostage until he gave me power enough to rule the world. He got really, REALLY pissed and turned me inside out. He told me if I could get rid of all of my patients, I could at least have my skin back. Then he'd probably give me some sort of power to make life easier for me."

"Gotta say… that's kind of shitty and definitely a reason to feel bad." says Kerry.

"What's the end game here though? What's the why?" asks Lucy.

"He said he was bored… I guess." says Uriah with a shrug.

"That makes sense. Torturing all the time would get a little old." Says Kerry looking over at the chunk of wood Lucy is holding. He nods in Uriah's direction after making eye contact with Lucy.

"Did you just tell her to hit me with that?" Says Uriah, whose feelings have been deeply hurt.

"No! Never!" says Kerry.

Lucy takes a step forward and hits Uriah on the forehead with the wood. His head jerks back and the worms swarm the wood and rip it out of Lucy's hand.

"See, that was just fucking mean!" says Uriah.

A door opens at the other end of the room and a man comes in looking worn out.

"Oh my God! This place is insane!" says the newcomer.

"Oh! I have to kill you yadda yadda… anyway." Says Uriah before the worms extend from his stomach. They surround the man and use their pincers to snip chunks of flesh off the man like scissors through putty. He falls into a pile of his own blood and discarded chunks of flesh, innards, and bone.

"Right. You're up next." Says Uriah turning to Kerry.

The worms lash out and Kerry feels one slice through his forearm. He jumps over to the side and hides behind a chair. His arm is cut deeply.

"That's a chair. I can cut through that!" says Uriah while proceeding to do that. Before he can get to Kerry, he feels something crush the back of his skull. He turns around to face Lucy, who is standing there brandishing a fire extinguisher. The worms move away from the chair and turn to her. Before they can attack Kerry is hitting Uriah in the back with one of the chairs.

"Damn it! Why can't you just play along and die!" Screams Uriah while receiving hits from the chair. "All I wanted was a test subject whose body was large enough to hold Satan. That's it. Instead, I get these mouthy fat ass-" Uriah's body explodes covering Kerry, Lucy, and the entire room in blood, gore, and little, tiny bits of bone.

A red mist hangs in the air from the explosion of Dr. Uriah Devers. A man walks through the mist with one hand in the pocket of his suit. He has a face that makes George Clooney look average and a figure that would make Jason Mamoa jealous.

"What an asshole." he says. "I told him if he made one more rude remark about the way someone looked… that was that."

"Awful polite of you." says Kerry.

"It's so cheap, you know? There are so many other things you can do to a person instead of calling them names. It's just so tacky and gross. Makes me cringe. I can't stand someone who bullies others with their words."

"Who are you exactly?"

"Satan. Lucifer. Beelzebub. The Morningstar. Wormwood. The Devvvviiiiilllll." While saying the last word he hits his hands on his head and makes horns with his finger while dancing around like a toddler.

"You caused all this!" yells Lucy.

"I got bored!"

"Are you going to kill us now in some horrible way?"

"Eh."

"What the fuck kind of answer is 'Eh?'"

"I'm kind of bored of this whole thing now."

"So… we can leave?" asks Kerry.

"Unless you want to stay here."

"No!"

"Then yeah, I don't care. Doors open."

They open the front door and Kerry pushes and turns back to Lucifer. "What about our money?" He asks.

"You can have all of the money now, I suppose."

"How many of us were there?"

"Five."

"Lucy, guy a minute ago, guy in waiting room, another random person,

Myself. I know where three of them are, but where are the other two?"

Satan nods over to two piles of flesh. Two bodies covered in lacerations. The skeletons have been torn from the bodies and placed sitting atop the masses of flesh like they're relaxing on a bean bag chair. One holds a Bible while the other appears to look on. They appear to be deep in conversation. Kerry recognizes one as the man he sat next to earlier in this same room.

"What the hell is that all about?" asks Lucy.

"Boredom." says Satan.

"Boredom." says Kerry.

"Boredom." says Lucy.

Satan walks toward them and pulls out a check book. He writes the amount of $10,000 on it.

"I'm giving you each $5000 for being so understanding." says Lucifer.

"Wow. I would say thanks but you've kind of ruined my life." says Kerry. Lucy nudges him in the side and takes the check. They close the door behind them and exit through another door at the end of the hallway.

"How are we going to explain all of that?" Asks Kerry when the bright sunshine hits his face.

No sooner than the question leaves his mouth the building they just exited goes up in an inferno.

"…oh." He says looking at the fire.

"What do you want to do now?" asks Lucy.

"Have you ever had Garlic Parmesan Bites from Domino's?" asks Kerry as they walk away from the blaze lightly taking each other's hands into their own.

"A couple of weirdos." says Lucy.

"A couple of weirdos." agrees Kerry.

NOTES:

My first romance story. Isn't that the kind of corny shit a horror writer should say about a gory story like this with a small love element to it? Truth be told, I don't know Kerry or Lucy, maybe they just want to be friends. Who's to say? I mean I wrote the thing so I guess I would be the one who could say, but you know what? Yeah. They fall in love and have like three kids or something. They go on vacation to Italy at some point. It's really cool; but I'm not writing a story about them in Italy when their son Dylan threw a breadstick at a waiter now am I?

HOLY DIVER

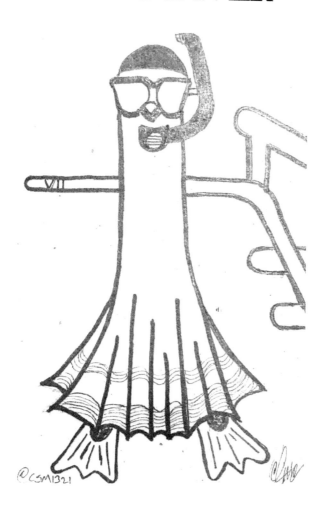

July 1987

Bayfield, Ohio

<u>MIGHT AS WELL JUMP! (JUMP!)</u>

It all started when that Jesus freak slipped on bacon grease and split his head open on the diving board. Personally, I would have checked the high dive before running out there and trying to do like seven backflips with a bunch of twists, or whatever the Hell he planned to do. He didn't get to do whatever that was. Instead, what he did accomplish was cracking open his head on the edge of the diving board and slowly rotating forward in his fall until his body hit the water with the loudest belly flop I have ever heard. Seriously, if he was alive when he hit, he wouldn't have been after, or he would have ralphed up whatever protein shake he drank that morning.

Here's the scoop, The Bayfield Lake Summer Camp always hosts The Jesus Bros, as I call them; I don't know the actual name of the group, who cares? The Jesus Bros are a group of super-buff, super oily, and super positive Christian guys who show up and do all these feats of strength to show how powerful God is. They rip phone books in half, they pick up twenty campers at a time, and one of them does tricks off the high dive.

Why Jesus, and or God would want anyone to rip a phone book in half, I have no idea; the lord works in mysterious ways and so forth.

We all rolled our happy camper asses out of bed at seven in the AM to go watch these goofballs do their thing. Seven AM is way too early in the morning to watch a guy rip a phone book in half when you can see it pretty much anytime on any college campus. The kids didn't seem to mind getting up that early though, they never do, they're like little balls of hyperactivity, whining, and hunger that their parents send to us for the summer. Being a counselor is such a mixed bag of bullshit, but the seven AM phone book disposal is the highest caliber of bullshit.

"Jessica Landon! PLEASE take my group to the lake for this. I do NOT want to leave." This was my best friend Abbey, who refuses to just call me "Jess" like everyone else here. She's the laziest person I ever met, yet somehow, she can put the work in to say my entire name. Really counterproductive to your overall persona, Abbey.

"Nope." I told her and kept walking.

"Why? Please. I will owe you."

"I took your group on the hike yesterday."

"And I appreciated it so, so much."

"Two days ago, I took them swimming."

"Another blessing."

"Then a day before that I took them to the cafe AND brought back your dinner."

"My lord and savior Jessica Landon, she does work miracles in my life."

"Yeah well, no miracles today. You get your lazy butt out here and come learn about breaking cinder blocks with your bare hands for a different lord and savior."

"You think they'll be as oily as last year?"

"Gotta say, probably more so."

That was the thought that got her butt in gear. Not the pay she was getting, not the fresh air, but the oily muscle men. I have to admit I was just as curious to see how much more baby oil the human body could hold on its surface as well, never know when you'll be trapped in a tight space with only a bottle of Johnson and Johnson's to get you to freedom.

The little event was the same as always; a bunch of Bible verses and dudes showing off how strong they were. In the middle of the event, one of the performers starts yelling from atop the high dive about how the Lord provided him with the gift of flipping.

That's right.

The gift of flipping.

He said it with such pride that I wanted to yell out "Hell yeah, Flipper!" but I was too irritated by how lame of a title his gift had to say anything.

He lists off a bunch of words for the trick he's about to do, pulls his goggles down, adjusts his little red speedo (Which, by the way, I found highly inappropriate to wear in front of a bunch of kids who were the average age of fourteen.) and ran to the edge of the high dive. He leaps into the air and lands on the end of the board, looking to use his momentum to send him flying off into Earth's orbit or something. Instead, his feet flew out from under him, and he smacked the back of his head on the diving board. Then the belly flop I spoke so highly of earlier took place. The other team members pulled his corpse up on the shore and started praying, not calling 911 or anything logical. I was pretty pissed about all that, so I went back to the main office and did it myself, I think I may have gotten a little huffy with the operator.

While I was there, I heard two other counselors, Shawn and Billy, come in freaking out and arguing.

"That was so perfect! It couldn't have gone any better! He busted his ass huge!" Shawn

"I just wish we could have seen more! He slipped and then we ran!" Billy.

I decided to step out and make my presence known at this point.

"Um, hi, yeah, you just killed that guy." I said.

"What?" asked Shawn with his jaw agape.

"He kind of hit his head really hard. He's also very dead."

They both stared at me, they started talking at once about how it was a prank, and they didn't mean for it to happen that way. They explained that Billy fell on bacon grease while cleaning the kitchen, so they decided to have a laugh. Shawn was really way too happy to admit it was his idea. Billy kept saying he wished they could have gotten more people first because now they'll probably be in jail.

Uh, yeah, Billy. That's usually what happens to people who kill someone.

Only that's not at all what happened. They decided to go into hiding in the woods that night to avoid being arrested. Super irritating because then it just made the rest of the night boring. All the kids were super scared and whiney too, most called their parents and left the next morning.

After loading about 87% of the camp's population into their parents' cars, or buses to go to their homes, the police came back from their search of the woods. They found Billy and Shawn no longer among the living. Shawn was nailed to a tree with his face pointed toward the stars, his chest had the words "Prideful Pete" carved into it.

Billy lay at his feet with his skin turned white. The police said it looked like he had drowned somehow. The killer carved "Greedy Gus" into his chest.

Pretty damn weird and scary. Another 9% of the campers left the next day. The other 4% of the campers must have had shitty parents.

IN THE MIDNIGHT HOUR, SHE CRIED MORE, MORE, MORE

I started to catch on when they found Ricky the next day. He was face down on the floor atop a bunch of soaking wet porno mags that he must have snuck in with him. I have no idea how he snuck in that much porn. He must have had a completely separate dumpster-sized duffel bag filled with it. "Here lies Ricky," I said shaking my head, "on a death bed of paper printed pubic hair."

"Poetic. You should speak at his funeral." said Abbey.

"I think I'll pass. The last time I even looked at Ricky the Pricky he was staring at my tits and saying 'wow! Bodacious boobies!' So, I think I'd just rather not go around him anymore."

"He's dead, though."

"Not even death can stop some men. Perversions from beyond the grave."

"How did he drown in the cafeteria?"

"Instead of spontaneous combustion, it was spontaneous drowning."

"Why are you so irritable? Somebody died. Like four people actually."

"And they ruined the whole summer! I'm kind of pissed!"

"What's with the little name?"

"Oh, you mean 'Lusty Larry' carved into his back?"

"Greedy Gus, Prideful Pete, not even their real names."

We both marinated in our silence for a bit until it hit me, and I yelled out "HOLY SHIT!" and pulled Abbey off the bed we were laying on. She complained, of course, physical exertion overcoming the single greatest light bulb moment I ever had.

I knew what was happening, this guy was killing people based on their sins. The seven deadly ones to be exact. Maybe he was one of those Jesus freaks and he hadn't left? Seeking revenge for the dead diver dipshit? All I could think was how we already found Pride, Greed, and Lust; so, as I was taught, the next in order would be Envy.

We both knew the only person at camp that would fit that bill was named Bill, only to stop confusion between himself and the other forty Bills or Billys at camp he changed his name to William, not Will, that pissed him off, had to hit all the syllables, about a week into camp.

William was always saying shit like "...Must be nice to have a car." or "I sure wish I had cool parents like that..." Jealous little annoying turd. He got under my skin with that stuff. One time I was talking about how I found a quarter by the vending machines, and he said "I wish I would find a quarter..." I gave him the damn quarter. Payphone costs fifty cents, the food here is free, what do I care if I can buy a can of Pepsi when I can get the same thing for free in the cafe? He didn't take the quarter either, started complaining about how he just wished he had good luck. Damnit, he was annoying, did I even want to try to save him?

I spoiled it because I just wrote that he WAS annoying and not he IS annoying. Yeah, we didn't make it in time. It was just after midnight and William was lying beside a tree, his foot tied to it by a rope, he clearly drowned somehow; the whole drowning on dry land thing was getting old, get a new gimmick, guy. William's hands were stretched out, reaching for a whole pile of things, books, watches, soda; it was a little on the nose honestly. So, on the nose in fact that the killer did not have to carve "Envious Erin" into his back. Isn't Erin the feminine spelling? I don't know, just seems like he could have used Eric, Ethan, or even Eugene to avoid that sort of confusion. Who am I to judge someone else's creativity though?

"Shit!" We both exclaimed, throwing our arms into the air.

No time to mourn. I guessed that at some point someone would find him, I didn't want to waste time with all the semantics of calling the cops and waking everyone up when I knew exactly where the killer was going next.

I have always picked on another counselor named Jillian about her eating. She was maybe ninety pounds soaking wet, which was a condition I hoped we wouldn't find her in. She could eat though; we're talking about eating five boxes of cereal in one sitting and not gaining an ounce level of metabolism here. I always told her it was like she had a portal to another dimension filled with souls possessed by the Wendigo; their hunger insatiable as they wait for Jillian's chewed-up food to fall out of the sky.

We headed to the cafeteria, Abbey complaining the whole way, too much hustle and bustle for her. We got there and Jillian was still kicking. I knew she would be there; midnight snacks were her favorite part of the day. She turned to look at us in surprise, half a dinosaur-shaped chicken nugget in her mouth.

"Pwease dun tal" she mumbled with her mouth full.

I explained how little we cared about her eating a Stegosaurus-shaped meat byproduct and led into the bit about the killer. She believed us, surprisingly. She just had to go use the restroom and then she'd go with us. We said yeah, sure, no harm no foul. Peeing is private, ya know? And neither of us had teeth to brush so we didn't want to interrupt. After about ten minutes of waiting and assuming the nuggets had done a number on her stomach, I realized exactly how stupid we were.

"You do realize we let the person we think is the next victim go off into the bathroom alone, right?" I asked standing up and trying to pull Abbey up off the bench we waited on.

"Yeah, I knew, I just needed a rest and thought, well, shit, if she doesn't think it's a big thing neither do I." She said standing up slower than I cared for a human to stand when one of their friends may be dead in a bathroom.

We found her drowned in a toilet, bags of dinosaur nuggets and junk food spread all over and around her.

"Gluttonous Gertrude" was her carving.

I stepped forward to try to help, knowing I was too late, and slipped on a Twinkie, of all things, a goddamned Twinkie. I looked up and saw a figure behind Abbey in the doorway wearing swimming goggles, a swimming cap, a blue speedo, and for some weird reason a snorkel.

He said "Flub glub gurgle blub mug tun."

I said, "Can't hear you through your snorkel!" as I grabbed Abbey's leg and pulled it out from under her, she fell backward into the man causing him to hit his head on the concrete wall.

At this point, Abbey decided she was good and rested up and ran as fast as she could out of the building entirely. I followed behind her telling her to slow down. If I could catch up and wait on her, I'd surely be with the person he planned to kill for Sloth. No way around it, as much as I loved her lazy ass, Abbey was going to be on his radar. Being my best friend, I was going to stick with her and try to save her. I said a quick prayer for whoever was going to bite the dust over anger, hoping they were angry enough to fuck Scuba Steve up before he got them. I couldn't help them; my hands were tied. I finally caught up to Abbey at the edge of the pool house, she was just staring at the swimming pool in shock. I shook her out of it and told her I had one Hell of an idea.

THE FINAL COUNTDOWN WEE-DEE DOO-DOO

"How long do I have to keep doing these laps?" Abbey shouted from the pool, "I'm getting really tired."

"Just keep swimming around!" I hissed through my teeth; this plan was never going to work if she didn't shut up.

I have no idea how much time, or how many times Abbey sighed before I heard something slapping on the ground off in the darkness. It sounded like someone was slapping the ground with a giant fly swatter. I made a shush hand gesture at Abbey and walked around the fence line with the small boat oar I took. I had it ready to Babe Ruth this aquatic asshole's head all the way to the Pacific when I stepped in a wet puddle. I squatted down; it was a flipper print. This guy was wearing flippers.

Who the Hell does that?

I heard the slapping off toward the opening in the fence, the slapping of flippers on the dry ground. I ran as quietly as I could around to the entrance to see him sneaking up to the pool behind Abbey, who was swimming in the opposite direction.

"Got you now, you snorkel-wearing son of a bitch!" I shouted while swinging the oar as hard as I could. Instead of meeting the back of his head as I intended, it hit his forearm and he snatched it from me. He kicked his leg out and caught me in my stomach knocking me to the ground.

"Blurb glub trug," he started while holding the oar over his head, "glub glug glug."

"Listen! I! Can't! Under! Stand! A! Word! You! Are! Saying!" I shouted each syllable as its own separate tiny little curse, hoping there was a witch or wizard somewhere in my bloodline and I had just enough magic in me to kill this guy.

He stopped and stared at me for a minute like he was confused. At this point a beach ball came flying from the direction of the pool and clocked him in the side of the head, knocking the snorkel from his mouth and causing him to drop the oar.

I scrambled to my feet and grabbed the oar, our positions had switched, I was now standing over him in the same way he was over me just a few seconds before.

"Sorry!" Abbey yelled, "I stopped doing laps long enough to nail him. I'll keep going now!"

At this point, I thought the plan was a little outdated but if Abbey was doing something physical consistently, I wasn't going to bother her.

"WAIT!" The man yelled holding both hands up to me. "You both have broken my curse!"

"Ugh. A curse. Of course. Why a curse?" I asked, still holding the oar.

"When those kids killed me, I came back to avenge my death. I had to save you all from the sins you were committing! That was the only way I could pass on to the afterlife and see the pearly gates!"

"Wait, what?"

"You cured your sin of Anger when you patiently waited for me to arrive instead of rushing off in anger. Your friend has cured her Sloth by being diligent in her swimming!"

"Bullshit-liar-man! You didn't even give the other five people a chance to save themselves! This is some lame-ass ploy to get me to call the cops so you can go to prison instead of getting your head split open by this here oar!"

"No, no, I swear! I died that day on the lake!"

"You're not even wearing the same color speedo! You're the phone book guy! I understand you're pretty mad about what happened... wait... see, it doesn't make sense! Am I a little crabby and cranky? Yes. It is summer and I'm stuck here watching all these little snots, which have all left now because of you, by the way. But I am NOT angry enough to kill seven people! That's vengeance, that's worse than me by a mile!"

He looked around and I could tell he knew the gimmick had run its course. He yelled "I must repent!" Then leaped up like a frog and ran towards the boathouse, I assume trying to make one last run at escaping.

He tripped over something and went down hard on the ground; I heard the front of his face connect with the concrete lip of the pool make a thud and cracking sound before his lifeless body rolled into the water.

"HEY!" was also heard in Abbey's voice at the same time. I looked and saw he tripped over her, she must have given up and crawled out of the pool to lay on the side.

"Listen," she said, "I am sorry, but you had me still swimming. He was occupied! Why couldn't I take a little rest?"

"It doesn't matter," I said nodding to the body floating face down, "he's a goner."

"Hell of a dive."

"Yep."

"Must have needed a drink."

"Must have."

"Really learned how to face down his problems."

"He sure did."

"Looks like swimming lessons are canceled."

"Probably so."

"He's a fish out of water."

"Alright, that one doesn't make sense. He is literally in the water."

Abbey shrugged.

I walked back up to the head counselor's office to tell him what had happened. I went alone, everyone knows these guys are never dead the first time around.

When the cops and paramedics showed up, I went with them to the pool to Abbey. She was just sitting there with her feet in the water like there wasn't a dead body floating around in the red water.

"Oh, hi!" she exclaimed, "I'm pretty sure he's dead, he started moving a little so I thwacked him with the oar, must have been his body letting out some gas because it smelled like rotten eggs."

"Thanks for that lovely information." Said a clearly frustrated Police officer.

We both went home the next day; camp was closed for the next two summers until someone else decided to open it. It shut down that summer because the kids kept saying they heard those flippers slapping around at night in their cabins. The next summer they tried to open it again, but no one wanted to go to a camp with a ghost that wore a speedo, I understood that logic pretty well. I keep in touch with Abbey, sometimes I've even been able to get her out of her bedroom to go for a hike believe it or not.

This past Christmas we were opening our gifts together and we came across one neither of us had brought. It was damp like it had sat out in the rain all day. We both slowly opened it and found a picture inside placed safely inside a waterproof Ziploc baggie. The picture was a different man dressed in the same outfit, only with a red speedo. He was holding a severed head and waving to the camera. There was a note on the back.

"I'm wearing the right color speedo now. See you next summer."

NOTES:

I love comedic slashers. Happy Death Day is my favorite "Slasher" ever made. I put some tributes in this for HDD, because what's a good slasher without some nods to the classics? I just said Happy Death Day was a classic in a roundabout way and you aren't going to disagree. Well, you COULD, but you'd have to tweet it or something and is it really worth all of that for me to just respond with "Yeah, well, whatever. K thx."
This story is also a tribute to my least favorite thing I have ever had to watch MULTIPLE times. That weirdo team of powerlifters who came to my middle school and talked about a guy having to kill his son in the gears of a train, and something about an elephant being chained up.
Pretty goddamned bleak content for a Christian weightlifting crew!

THANKEE!
It's six stories so I'm just going to make some lists!

Breanna Spencer- My favorite person to tell me not to do things that I do anyway and then have to admit she was right.

Sasha Banks/Mercedes Varnado- Thankee for inspiring me to be the best person I can be, and to create the things I want to create.

AUTHORS WHO RULZZZ THAT YOU SHOULD READ!
Sarah Jane Huntington, CJ Sampera, Kyra Torres, Coy Hall, Christopher Robertson, Brian Berry, Brittany Johnson, Derek Hutchins, Jeremy Megargee, DM Guay, Catherine McCarthy, Adam Hulse, Harriet Everend, HD Scarberry, Joseph Slater, Joshua Marsella, Sabrina Voerman, Brooklyn Dean, Elford Alley, Kool Guy Kyle Winkler, Garth Jones, ME Grey, Wendy Dalrymple, Braedon Riddick, Lorien Lawrence, Spencer Hamilton, Felix ID Dimaro, and if I forgot you, IM SORRY OK? JUST WRITE YOUR NAME HERE_____ AND SEND ME A DM SO I CAN FIX IT NEXT TIME.

PEOPLE THAT RULLZZZZZ
Eric Pierce, Nikki Pierce, Nora Pierce, Cody Lambert, Jeremiah Cullen, Crystal Cotrill,

Jesse Mowery, Jake Kennedy, Josh Kennedy, Bridgett Kennedy, Shrub at Goblinhaus, Casey Smallwood, Chris McCormick, Emily Gibson Cardwell, Nichi at Dark Between Pages, Caleb The Bookeyman, Eric ,Kristina Osborne @ Truborn Design, Missy Kritzer, Olivia Allison, Josh @ Working Man Reads, BrainBleedZine, The Big Cheese Andrew Robert @ Darklit Press, Joe @ Cryptoteeology, Kelli Maroney, Dawn D&T Publishing, and anyone I forgot, IM SORRY AND WRITE YOUR NAME HERE LIKE THE AUTHORS I FORGOT

<u>ABOUT THE DUMB ASS WHO WROTE THIS</u>

Damien Casey used to be a manatee.
He found a weird book in some seaweed one time.
He read the the words.
The words were Danzig lyrics.
Now he's an evil manatee who lives in WV.
It's sorta like The Little Mermaid.
Only not at all.
About the author parts are the worst.
K thx.
Instagram- @Damienthulhu
Twitter- @dcuglybooks

ALSO BY DAMIEN CASEY

Aphid
Stories Christians don't have to Read
Backwards
PUP
51
The Village of Gill(Choose your own
Adventure)
Coffin Dodger

COMING SOON
Hot Pink Satanism/With Kyra R. Torres
Appalachian Dinosaur Cult

Printed in Great Britain
by Amazon